THE
POINTLESS
LEOPARD

THE POINTLESS LEOPARD

What Good Are Kids Anyway?

Colas Gutman

Illustrated by Delphine Perret

Translated from the French by
Stephanie Seegmuller

PUSHKIN CHILDREN'S BOOKS

Pushkin Children's Books
71–75 Shelton Street, London WC2H 9JQ

Original title: *L'enfant*
Text by Colas Gutman and illustrations by Delphine Perret
© 2011 L'école des loisirs, Paris

English translation © 2014 by Stephanie Seegmuller
(Translated by Stephanie Seegmuller with a little help from
her friends, Daniel Seton and Gesche Ipsen)

This translation first published by Pushkin Press in 2014

ISBN 978 1 782690 40 5

Text designed and set in 13 / 23 Chaparral
by Tetragon, London

Printed in China by WKT Co

www.pushkinpress.com

To my mother

"I don't like it in the country, it's ugly, it's green and it's boring!"

"Leonard, you can't say that! It's wonderful in the country!" said Mum.

"That's right, all children love it in the country," said Dad.

"Well, not me."

At the weekend, what my parents like to do above all is drink tea in front of an open fire, listening to the silence. They call this country life. It's horrible.

Me, what I like to do is walk on the pavement, jump on benches, go to the cinema, and run after the pigeons. In the country there's nothing to do, except: admire. It's the same as being bored, but with your eyes wide open.

So I'm allowed to get bored in front of the open fire, the ducks, the hens, the trees and sometimes the tractors, which go by in slow motion.

When Dad and Mum aren't drinking tea around the fire like cavemen, they take me for a walk. Most of the time it's raining, it makes your feet hurt and it makes you thirsty. It's worse than anything.

But last weekend, something finally happened.

"Look how beautiful it is!" said Mum.

"It's not beautiful, it's green," I said.

"That's because of all the rain," said Dad.

"Yes, it rains all the time," I said.

"What about taking this track?" said Mum.

A track is a street without shops, and with grass in the middle, stones that make you twist your ankles, and stinging nettles at the sides.

My parents love walking along tracks they don't know. They say they're magical places.

Mum said:

"I'm sure there are hens on this track."

"Seeing all these animals running free – it's really heart-warming," said Dad.

Me, I thought of the tigers, the bears and the monkeys that are printed on my duvet, and I stepped into a big puddle.

While Dad was counting the leaves of a tree and Mum was wondering whether it was the season for chestnuts, I ran into a sheep.

Because I'm polite, I said hello. And because this sheep talked, it replied:

"Hi."

And he added:

"Excuse me, but what are you?"

"What do you mean, what am I?" I said.

"Well, what kind of animal are you?"

I thought, "Wow, I'm really out in the middle of nowhere like Mum said. Poor sheep, he's never seen a kid in his life!"

"I'm not an animal," I said, "I'm Leonard."

"Is it like a leopard?" asked the sheep.

"Nope, it's my name. What about you? What are you called?"

"Sheep."

"I see."

That's when the sheep had a sniff at me and asked a funny question:

"And what are you for?"

So I thought of a bunch of things:

a bottle-opener

a sewing machine

a blender

a football

a pillow

I turned to the sheep and I said:

"I don't think I'm for anything."

The sheep started laughing so hard that a cow came along.

"What's that?" asked the cow.

"It's a sort of pointless leopard," said the sheep.

"Noo, I'm a kid! Ok, listen, I'm going to
get my parents and they'll explain everything,
because you're just driving me nuts!"

Here's another thing about the country,
though—you get lost all the time. Nothing looks
more like a track than another track, a tree just
looks like a tree, and a stone like a stone.

I was lost, like when I'm in the department store, but this time there was no meeting point where someone could come and pick me up.

So I stayed with the cow and the sheep, then a hen came along. They sat cross-legged, which for the cow was a bit tricky, and they said:

"Tell us what a Leonard is."

"You mean a child?"

"Yes."

That put me in a state, a bit like when it's my birthday, and I'm trying to guess what all the presents are inside their wrapping paper.

I thought: "A child's not a can opener or a hair dryer, and not a pack of crisps either."

Then I said:

"A child goes with parents. A bit like batteries and a remote-controlled car."

"You're a battery?" asked the cow.

"Er, no, not really."

"So you don't have a use," said the hen.

All of a sudden, I really felt like changing the hen into a roast chicken and eating it with chips.

But then I thought of Dad, who always says that when you get angry, you should listen to silence and everything will sort itself out.

Although things didn't sort themselves out because the cow started showing off. It said:

"You see, take me—I make tasty milk and cheese!"

And the hen said:

"And I lay fresh eggs!"

And the sheep:

"And I make nice knitted cardigans!"

Then the three said together:

"We all have a use!"

"Listen, I make pasta necklaces for my Mum and give hugs to my Dad."

"That sounds pretty rubbish," said the hen.

"Ok, you're getting on my nerves! Anyway, kids are much better than animals, everyone knows that. And I know stuff, and you don't!"

"Oh yes? And what do you know for instance?" said the sheep.

So, right in front of them, I made a list of the things I knew:

The Earth is not flat

$97 + 3 = 100$

I before E, except after C.

I'm not allowed to bring a mobile phone to school

"And what's the point of knowing all that?" asked the hen.

"Er. I'm not sure," I said.

But in school they often say all that will be useful later on. Then I had a brainwave. I said:

"The point of a child is to become someone later on!"

"That sucks," said the cow.

"Gobbledygook," said the sheep.

"Bah," said the hen, "we're interested in you now, not later."

So, only half-believing it, I said:

"The point of a kid is doing homework, taking the rubbish out and mowing the lawn!"

"Whatever," said the cow.

"That's stupid," said the sheep.

"Ridiculous," said the hen, "no really, you have no point at all."

And that made me sad. Like when I get bad marks in spelling, Maths and in Art, all on the same day.

But then the hen asked:

"What do you know about wolves?"

"Not much. In the city there're mainly dogs and pigeons."

"We know one. Maybe he knows what you're good for... Want to meet him?"

"Sure, if he can help me."

That's how we walked down another track, which looked like the twin brother of the first one.

The hen shouted:

"Wolf, we're bringing you a city kid! Bon appetit!"

So I understood that it was a trap, especially when the cow said:

"This one is particularly stupid, he thought we'd never seen children before!"

"That we were country bumpkins," said the hen.

"Ha ha, that's a good one," said the wolf. "But hold on, I only eat the finest quality children. The last one you brought me wasn't very tasty."

And the wolf started to size me up:

"Oh, my child, what small hands you have!"

"Yes, all the better to poke you in the eye with if you lay a hand on me," I said.

"And what small ears you have!"

"Yes, so you don't get me confused with an elephant."

"And what a small mouth you have!"

"All the better to scream with," I said.

"What's wrong with this child, he's not afraid of wolves?!"

"Well I'm a city kid. I'm afraid of dogs, not wolves."

The cow talked to the sheep, and the hen to the wolf and then the four of them looked at me with strange eyes and the sheep said:

"Bite him in the legs!"

"If I had teeth, I'd start with the arms, they look plump and tasty," recommended the hen.

"The bum, the bum, the bum," shouted the cow.

That's when I started to be scared, like the day I thought there was:

a burglar in the living room
a monster under my bed
another one in my cupboard
Brussels sprouts for dinner.

But then the wolf sniffed me and said:

"Yuck! This kid is completely polluted.
He smells like exhaust fumes and genetically-
modified chicken! I don't want to make myself ill
by eating a city kid, take him away!"

So I thought: "That's it then, I really have no point at all. Even the wolf doesn't want to eat me."

"Do you want to be taken back to your parents?" offered the hen.

"Bah..."

"Come on, I'm sure they're very worried," said the hen.

"They must be looking for you all over," said the sheep.

"Doubt it."

Then I cried as hard as the day I banged my head, bit my tongue and twisted my thumb all at the same time.

"Oh, he's all sad," said the cow.

"Do you want to sing 'Baa Baa Black Sheep'?" suggested the sheep.

"Or 'Old MacDonald Had a Farm'," asked the cow.

"Or 'Hickety Pickety My Red Hen'?" asked the hen.

"Noo, leave me alone!"

"We could be friends, if you like," said the sheep.

"I'm not friends with traitors who trap kids!"

"We won't do it again," said the hen.

"We promise," said the cow.

"That's right," said the sheep.

"Listen, you're nice and everything, but you did all say I was pointless. So leave me alone."

Then I went off, alone, deep into the countryside, without looking back.

I thought: "I'm going to be like Mowgli, I'll eat roots and acorns, and I'll talk to the trees."

But then in the country, when you start listening to silence, there's always some noise. In the distance, I heard the siren of a fire engine.

So I was hopeful again.

Maybe my parents are looking for me after all.

Maybe they've raised a kidnapping alert. I must be on TV right now. All my friends are watching me, they're showing the photo where I have my cowboy hat on.

So I ran as fast as I could toward the siren noise, I went by a tree that looked like another tree, and I took a track that looked like another track and then there was a miracle, like when Mum bought crisps, lemonade and Nutella on the same day: I saw my parents.

They were doing something typically country-like which is even more boring than listening to silence, they were sleeping under a tree.

The fire engine siren wasn't for me. So I cried like on the day I was cutting some onions and sprayed lemon juice in my eyes.

When Dad and Mum finally woke up, I
thought they'd just throw me in the bin. In the
country, they call it the dump, but they said:

"So, Leonard, have you had fun?"

"Did you look at any ants?"

"Did you find any fun sticks?"

"No way, I had a chat with a hen, a sheep, a cow and even a wolf."

"Ah, these kids, such imagination!" said Dad.

But I stayed as quiet as an earthworm.

By that night, oddly, they still hadn't thrown me away. I thought maybe they were waiting to have other stuff to put in the bin, so they could make a whole bag of it.

But then I couldn't wait anymore. So I asked:

"What's the point of a child?"

"No point," said Dad, laughing.

And Mum said:

"And really, children aren't supposed to have a use at all!"

So I thought: "A kid should not be a table mat, a can opener or a corkscrew – that's a start."

And then I smiled, and I looked at the open fire, and listened to the silence.

PUSHKIN CHILDREN'S BOOKS

Just as we all are, children are fascinated by stories. From the earliest age, we love to hear about monsters and heroes, romance and death, disaster and rescue, from every place and time.

In 2013, we created Pushkin Children's Books to share these tales from different languages and cultures with younger readers, and to open the door to the wide, colourful worlds these stories offer.

From picture books and adventure stories to fairy tales and classics, and from fifty-year-old bestsellers to current huge successes abroad, the books on the Pushkin Children's list reflect the very best stories from around the world, for our most discerning readers of all: children.